Norman to the Rescue

Written by
Loren Spiotta-DiMare

Illustrated by
Kara Lee

in loving memory of my hero, Joseph Bertrand Spiotta
~ Loren Spiotta-DiMare

for my cats, Mocha, "Dokey Doodle" and Inky, "Ink Spot", two precious little souls who have blessed my life with unconditional love and friendship. You're both in my heart forever.
~ Kara Lee

Doris Day Animal Foundation

SEASIDE
REALTY
THE MOCHA CAFE
LIBERTY

The lost yellow dog wandered through the streets. He peeked in windows, stood in open doorways and watched passersby, searching for his owner. Each day he became more confused. The speeding cars and honking horns frightened him. He'd never been so hungry. His stomach growled. There were wonderful smells floating in the air from a restaurant. He sat by the door waiting for a handout, but he was chased away.

One morning, a police officer offered the sad-looking stray a piece of his breakfast roll. The dog lunged at the buttery bread and wagged his whole rear end. The officer laughed. "Hop in," he said. "I'll take you for a ride." The yellow dog leaped into the van and pushed his nose against the window.

When the van stopped, the yellow dog followed the officer past a long row of cages filled with dogs. Most barked as he was led to the last cage. 'Clang!!' The door slammed shut. The yellow dog jumped and began to howl. "Don't leave me here. Come back!" he seemed to say.

Day after day visitors walked through the Seaside Police Station's Animal Shelter. But no one stopped for long. The officer fed and talked to the lonely dog, often reaching to scratch his ears. "We haven't found your home, and no one has asked to adopt you," the officer whispered one afternoon, sounding worried.

The next morning, a young man entered the shelter. Most of the dogs wagged their tails and barked. The yellow dog just sat and stared. As the man turned away, the dog barked once as if to say, "Come back here."

The man returned and pushed his hand through the bars to pat the dog. "Don't let anything happen to him," he said to the officer. "I'm coming back with my wife."

Annie was working alone, thinking about her dog, Lulu, who was getting too old to come to the shop. Suddenly, her husband burst through the door. "Let's go, Annie," yelled Steve. "We have to rescue a dog." Before she knew it, they were leaving the shelter with the yellow dog. "He'll be company for you at the store and a pal for Lulu," Steve said.

When they arrived home, Lulu bounded out to greet them. She sniffed the newcomer from the top of his nose to the tip of his tail. "I think they're going to be good friends," Annie said. Then she bent down to pet both dogs. "Let's take them to the beach and stretch their legs."

By the river leading into the sea, it was safe to let the dogs off their leashes. The yellow dog raced along the beach and jumped high into the air. Annie and Steve laughed aloud. Soon the dogs were splashing through the water together, wrestling with a great big stick.

Annie and Steve thought of different names for the yellow dog. Nothing seemed quite right. Watching a movie one night, they saw a golden brown calf named Norman. "Norman!" they giggled together. "Let's call him Norman."

Norman loved going to the shop with Annie. When a customer had a question, she'd reply, "I don't know. I'll have to ask the boss," and tap the counter with her hand. On cue, Norman would stand up, place his paws on the counter and bark. It always brought a laugh.

At home, Annie and Steve played lots of games with the dogs. Frisbee and soccer were Norman's favorites. When someone rolled a ball to him, he'd push it back with his nose. Lulu was always nearby, eager to join in the fun.

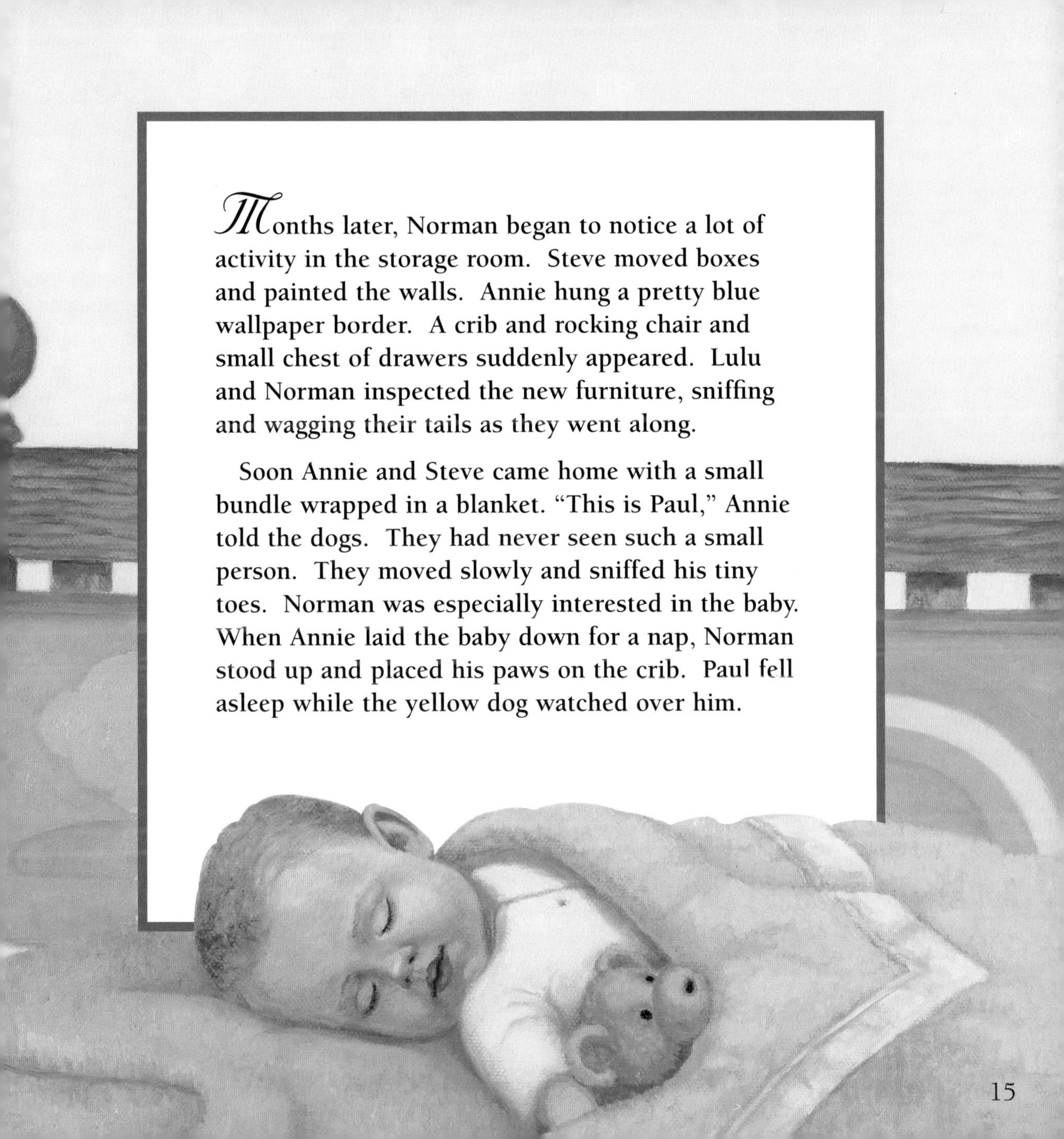

Months later, Norman began to notice a lot of activity in the storage room. Steve moved boxes and painted the walls. Annie hung a pretty blue wallpaper border. A crib and rocking chair and small chest of drawers suddenly appeared. Lulu and Norman inspected the new furniture, sniffing and wagging their tails as they went along.

Soon Annie and Steve came home with a small bundle wrapped in a blanket. “This is Paul,” Annie told the dogs. They had never seen such a small person. They moved slowly and sniffed his tiny toes. Norman was especially interested in the baby. When Annie laid the baby down for a nap, Norman stood up and placed his paws on the crib. Paul fell asleep while the yellow dog watched over him.

The house became a lot busier with Paul's arrival. There seemed to be diapers, bottles and baby toys all over the place. Annie and Steve made sure to give Norman and Lulu plenty of attention so they wouldn't become jealous of the baby. But there was no need to worry – both liked their little friend. When Paul cried, Norman followed Annie to the crib. He sat next to her while she rocked and fed the baby. When he was done, Norman nosed Annie to make sure she put Paul back in his crib.

One day, rounding a corner, Norman bumped into the wall. "That's odd," Annie thought. A few weeks later, Steve tossed the Frisbee and Norman missed it. As the dogs walked along the beach, the yellow dog leaned against Lulu. "Something's not right," Annie said to Steve as she watched the dogs. "I'm going to take Norman to the vet."

"He's running into things," Annie explained to Dr. Glaser, "and he doesn't always catch his ball."

The vet examined Norman, paying special attention to his eyes. Looking up, she said, "Norman is going blind."

"Will he be able to see at all?" Annie asked in a frightened voice. "Can anything be done to help him?"

"No. He has a disease that can't be cured," the vet responded. "He will lose his sight slowly, like a candle burning out. One day the light will be gone. I'm sorry."

Trying not to cry, Annie brought Norman home.

"I have sad news," Annie explained to Steve that evening. "The vet said Norman is going blind."

"Oh no!" Steve exclaimed. "Would surgery help?"

"No," Annie replied softly. "There's nothing we can do."

Steve hugged his wife. Then they both hugged Norman. "Don't worry Annie. Plenty of blind people and dogs have happy lives." Norman stood up and barked. Steve and Annie laughed. "He's the same old Norman," Steve said. "He'll be fine."

As Norman slowly lost his sight, Annie and Steve were careful not to move the furniture. That way, Norman would remember where it was placed. He soon learned to move around the house without bumping into things. When Steve rolled a soccer ball to Norman's nose, he could roll it back. Annie gave him an old plastic milk carton to play with. It was easier for Norman to hear as it slid across the floor and just as much fun as a tennis ball.

Best of all, Norman could still romp on the beach. If he ran too close to driftwood, Annie would yell out, "Easy!" so he would be careful.

1%
LOWFAT
½ GALLON

One day, Annie's mother came for a visit. The two women decided to take pictures of Paul at the beach. Lulu was napping, but Norman joined them. As they walked along the shore, two children splashed happily in the water.

Without warning, a dangerous riptide developed and began to pull the children out to sea. Both started to scream. The boy was able to swim to shore, but his sister wasn't strong enough to fight the tide. She thrashed in the water, shouting for help. No one seemed to hear.

Norman trotted along the shore. Then a faint sound caught his attention. He stopped and perked his ears.

Suddenly Norman dropped his stick and tore down the beach. Fearing he would hurt himself, Annie yelled for him to stop. But he ignored her and jumped right into the river.

Norman fought against the current and swam toward the girl's cries. She grabbed hold of his collar and he started to swim to shore. But the exhausted girl lost her grip. Norman swam frantically in circles trying to find her again.

Annie reached the water's edge and saw the girl in trouble. She was a poor swimmer, so she couldn't help the drowning child.

"His name is Norman. Call his name! He'll help you," Annie shouted.

The girl cried, "NORMAN! NORMAN!" Norman found her again. This time she held on tight. Norman tugged her all the way to shore.

The young girl was shaking when she reached the beach. Annie wrapped her in a towel.

"His eyes looked like two headlights coming to save me," the girl said.

"Norman's blind," Annie explained.

"He's my guardian angel," the girl replied, and threw her arms around him.

The girl's parents and brother came running up. "Lisa, Lisa, are you all right?" her mother cried out.

Lisa ran into her arms. "Norman saved me from drowning. He can't see, but he saved my life." Speechless, the woman hugged Lisa and stroked the blind yellow dog.

News of the heroic rescue traveled fast. Articles about Norman appeared in newspapers and magazines. Reports were heard on radio and TV. An animal shelter named him '*Animal Hero of the Year*,' and awarded him a medal.

Months later Lisa went to visit Norman. Annie, Steve and the dogs met Lisa and her family at the door with lots of hugs and kisses. "It's great to see you all again," Annie said. "Why don't we go for a picnic down by the river?" As they headed for the beach, Norman ran out in front, barking wildly as he splashed through the water, grabbing a big stick along the way.

Glossary

	Page	
adopt	7	to choose to take home as a member of a family
bundle	15	a package
burst	9	break through suddenly
confused	2	mixed-up
dangerous	22	could cause injury or harm
disease	18	a sickness
driftwood	20	pieces of wood washed up on the beach
exhausted	27	very tired
faint	22	weak, distant or far away
favorites	13	things you like the most
heroic	30	brave
ignored	24	didn't pay attention to
passersby	2	people walking by
returned	9	came back
riptide	22	a strong flow of surface water pulling away from shore
romp	20	play
shelter	9	a safe place that cares for homeless animals
slammed	7	shut loudly
thrashed	22	swung one's arms and legs hard
tore	24	moved very fast
trotted	22	ran slowly, jogged

Artwork designed by Kara Lee
Book designed by Anita Soos Design

The real Norman

Lisa's parents were so indebted to Norman for saving their daughter's life that they offered to pay for surgery to restore his sight. Unfortunately a veterinary eye specialist confirmed there is no cure. Norman continues to live happily in his loving home by the sea. An additional percentage of sales from this story will support the Clatsop County Animal Shelter in Oregon, and help with Norman's health-care.

All dogs should wear collars and tags, so that if they do get lost, it will be possible to find their owners and send them home.

The Doris Day Animal Foundation is a nonprofit organization dedicated to the protection of animals. Through education, the DDAF aims to empower individuals and organizations to act on behalf of animals. National campaigns by the DDAF address pet overpopulation and humane education for children in grades K-7. The DDAF is working to bring legal, law enforcement, and mental health professionals together over issues of cruelty and violence toward animals and people. With increased care and respect for animals, we may develop greater compassion for each other. For more information about the Doris Day Animal Foundation, call (202) 546-1761.

Published by The Benefactory, Inc., 925 N. Milwaukee Avenue, Suite 1010, Wheeling, IL 60090. The Benefactory produces books, tapes and toys that foster animal protection and environmental preservation. For more information, call: (847) 919-1777, or visit our website, www.readplay.com

ISBN 1-58021-053-8
10 9 8 7 6 5 4 3 2 1

printed on recycled paper